Pee Wee
Goes to School

Tanya Renee Gentry

Fulton Books, Inc.
Meadville, PA

Published by Fulton Books 2020

ISBN 978-1-64654-066-2 (paperback)
ISBN 978-1-64654-830-9 (hardcover)
ISBN 978-1-64654-067-9 (digital)

Printed in the United States of America

Dedication

I dedicate this book to all the sickle-cell Warriors in the world. Stay strong, your health is your wealth, take care of yourself. You have a purpose here on earth, the strength you hold is incredible. Once you find your purpose you will be unstoppable. You can be and do anything you put your mind to, you are champions. Lead with love and live life to the fullest.

1

"Hi, my name is Pee Wee! I'm so excited I'm going to a new school tomorrow! Everything has to be perfect: pants, check. Shirt, check.

Socks and shoes? Check. Now I'm ready for school tomorrow!

My dad's in the military, so we have to move sometimes and I have to attend a new school.

It's no fun when I have to leave my friends, but my dad says, "Life is about change, so keep moving forward."

I have an older sister named Jada, who's going to the same school, just a different grade. I'm sure glad my sister will be with me.

*****

"Pee Wee, we're going to go to your school a little early tomorrow so I can speak with your teacher about your sickle cell anemia and your needs," said Pee Wee's mom.

"Okay, Mom."

"My mom's a nurse, and she loves taking care of people. Sometimes she has to take extra care of me because I have sickle cell anemia."

"*What's* sickle cell, *you may ask?*

Good question!

Sickle cell *is a red blood cell disorder.*

Sometimes my blood cells become sticky and clump together.

When this happens, it's called a pain crisis and I might have to go to the hospital."

"At the hospital, I have to have oxygen, an IV, and medication to feel better. The problem is the sickle cells do not carry enough oxygen through my body."

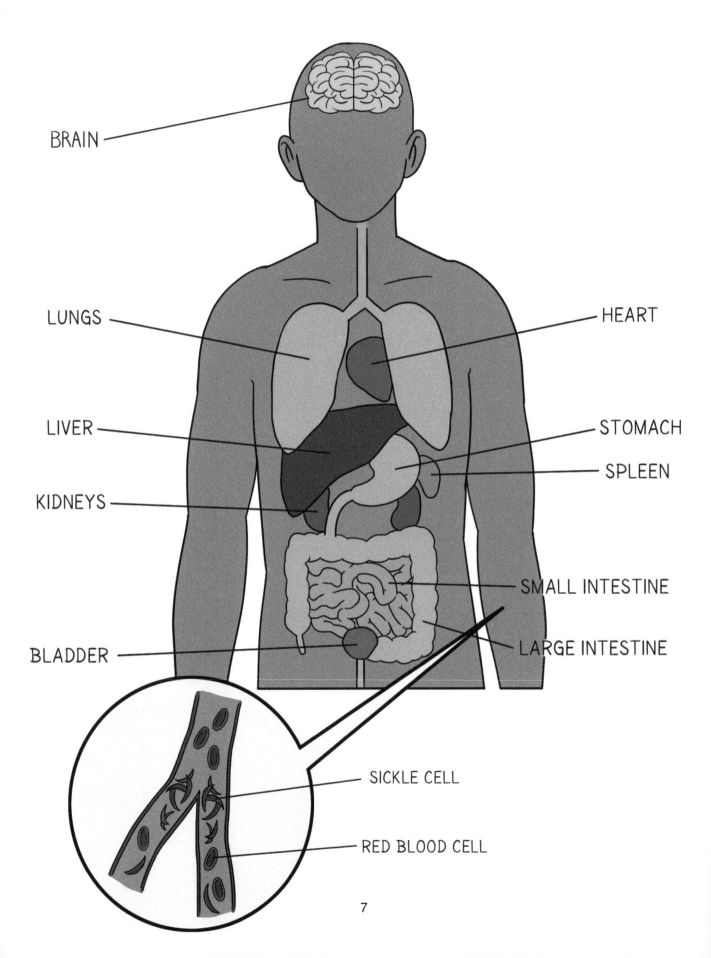

BRAIN

LUNGS

LIVER

KIDNEYS

BLADDER

HEART

STOMACH

SPLEEN

SMALL INTESTINE

LARGE INTESTINE

SICKLE CELL

RED BLOOD CELL

7

A lack of oxygen can affect my vital organs. Vital organs are the parts inside our bodies, like our hearts; that make us able to run, jump, and play.

I'm just like you, but I have things I have to do to stay healthy. Like, drink plenty of water, eat a balanced diet, exercise and sometimes take medicine.

"Sickle cell is not who I am. It's just a part of my life I have to deal with."

After dinner, the night before his first day at his new school, Pee Wee got ready for bed.

He said his prayer and then jumped into bed, excited for the big day!

The next morning, Pee Wee woke up and said, "I thought the morning would never come! Today is the big day! I'm going to my new school!"

"Good morning, Pee Wee," said Pee Wee's mom and dad.

"Good morning!"

"Are you ready for school?" his parents asked.

"Yes, I am!"

Pee Wee's dad replied, "Okay, remember what I told you. Change is good. Be yourself. You're an awesome person. You should have no problem making friends."

"Okay, Dad."

"Okay, have a good day. I'll see you tonight!" said Pee Wee's dad.

When Pee Wee walked outside, he felt the sun on his face and heard the birds chirping.

Upon arriving at school, Pee Wee jumped out of the car, ready for his day.

Once in the classroom, Pee Wee's mom greeted the teacher, "Good morning Ms. Philips, this is Pee Wee. He's in your class this year."

Ms. Philips smiled and said, "Hi, Pee Wee."

Pee Wee's mom looked to Ms. Philips and said, "We wanted to talk to you about Pee Wee's sickle cell and his needs to stay healthy, in order to have a good day." Pee Wee's mom went on to say, "Pee Wee will need to drink plenty of water throughout his day, which may cause him to have a few restroom trips. If he stays hydrated, he will be okay."

"He will be fine. He's in good hands," said Ms. Philips.

And with that, Pee Wee's mom left.

No one noticed the kid listening at the door.

Then, a group of kids on the playground started whispering to each other.

"That kid Pee Wee has sickle cell!"

"What's that?"

"I don't know, but he can't touch me!"

"Me either. He has the cooties!"

"Yeah, the cooties!"

Then the whispering got louder, and someone in the crowd said out loud, "That kid has the sickle cell cooties. Don't touch him!"

"I heard it's contagious!" said another.

Jada saw what was happening and said to the group of kids standing together, "my brother doesn't have cooties, and he's not contagious. He has sickle cell."

"He goes through a lot, and it's not funny. Just because he has to do things differently doesn't make him a bad person." Jada ended by saying, "You might make a new friend if you just gave him a chance."

This really hurt Pee Wee's feelings. He sat alone at recess.

Then the bell rang.

Once back in the class, Pee Wee just sat there.

He had never been treated like that before.

He wasn't sure what to do.

After school, Jada asked Pee Wee, "You okay?"

"Yeah."

"You sure?"

"Yeah."

"Are you feeling okay?" Jada asked.

"Yeah, I'm okay. Just tired!"

Pee Wee knew his sister was just being protective, but he didn't know what to say.

Once in the car Pee Wee's mom said, "Hey, guys, how was your day?"

"Good!" replied Jada.

"How was your first day of school, Pee Wee?"

"It was okay,"

"Just okay? What's wrong?"

Pee Wee just shrugged and said, "I don't know!"

"Talk to mommy, sweetheart. What's wrong?"

"The kids made fun of me, and no one likes me."

"Why do you say that?" Pee Wee's mom stopped and turned as she got out of the car and looked at him.

"Because of my sickle cell. They think I'm contagious and that I have the cooties!"

"What? Sickle cell is not contagious! It's hereditary you have to be born with it. Maybe we can talk to your teacher and the class about sickle cell so they understand you're just like them. You just have a few things you need to do to stay healthy."

"I don't know, Mom." Pee Wee wasn't sure.

"It's going to be okay," his mom replied.

"Okay" he replied, although he was not sure about this idea.

20

It was dinnertime, and Pee Wee's mom said, "Pee Wee, it really bothers me that you were bullied today!"

"Bullied?" Pee Wee asked.

"Yes, bullied. You were teased and made fun of. That's bullying!" said his mom.

"Pretty much," said Jada.

"When I was a young kid," Pee Wee's mom went on to say, "I used to walk to school with a group of kids in the neighborhood. There was a boy that teased my friend named Erica because she was a little bigger than him. He called her fat, pointed at her and laughed. One day, I just told him to leave her alone. I told him that it wasn't funny and to stop. I could tell it hurt her feelings. You know what? After that day, he never said anything else to her. She walked to school in peace. When I was young, I never thought that one person standing up for someone else would make a difference, but it did!"

Pee Wee's mom ended her story by saying, "You know you can make a difference too, Pee Wee."

The next day at school, no one spoke to Pee Wee.

"Guess it's going to be a long day!" He sighed.

But once at lunch, Pee Wee got a surprise: a kid he didn't know got his lunch and came and sat by him.

Even though they didn't speak a word, it felt good not to sit alone at lunch.

After school, Pee Wee ran to his mom's car with a big smile on his face, shouting, "Hi, Mom!"

"Hi, Pee Wee. How was your day?"

"It was good!"

"Good? Okay, that's better than yesterday," she replied.

"Yes, ma'am. A kid at school ate lunch with me today."

"Really? What's his name?"

"I don't know. We didn't talk much. We just ate lunch."

"Well, that's good, Pee Wee. Each day will get better. You're so charming. I can't wait for everyone to get to know you. The smart, kind, good-hearted, handsome guy I see every day! Just be yourself and talk about the things you like," she said.

"Thank you, Mom."

All of a sudden, Pee Wee was feeling more confident.

That night, Pee Wee said his prayers before bed as usual. He asked for strength to make him brave enough to walk into school the next day without being worried about the other kids.

When morning came, Pee Wee got up and got dressed for school. As he ate breakfast, he said to himself, "Today is going to be a good day!"

His sister Jada said, "If anyone messes with you, let me know."

Pee Wee smiled and said, "Okay."

He knew his older sister would always be there for him and protect him.

But he had a good feeling about the new day.

As Pee Wee walked into school, he heard someone say, "Hi, Pee Wee."

He turned around and saw the kid from the lunchroom the day before.

"Hi!" Pee Wee said with a smile on his face.

"Hi, Pee Wee," another kid said.

"Hi," Pee Wee replied.

All of a sudden, Pee Wee saw a lot of friendly faces.

As Pee Wee entered the classroom, he was confident that it was going to be a great day.

"Hi, Pee Wee," said a girl sitting in the front row.

"Hi," Pee Wee replied, smiling.

When lunch came, Pee Wee didn't know what to expect.

But as he got his lunch and sat at a table, the kids that spoke to him earlier in the day came and sat next to him. This time, introducing themselves.

"Hi, Pee Wee. I'm Charlie."

"I'm Sara."

"I'm Aiden!"

"Hi!" Pee Wee responded.

As they ate lunch, Charlie asked, "Hey, Pee Wee, do you like video games?"

"Yeah, that's my favorite thing to do after homework,"

"What's your favorite game to play?"

"Extreme sports and racing games."

Then Aiden joined in, saying, "Hey, football is one of my favorite games to play too!"

They all began to laugh and talk about their favorite part of the game and shared their highest scores. As Pee Wee looked around at everyone, talking and joking with one another, he remembered what his mom said, "*Just be yourself.*" And she was right!

Just then, Pee Wee's sister Jada walked into the lunchroom.

She saw that Pee Wee was not alone, and she thought to herself, "*Wow, my brother is actually having a great time, laughing and joking with his classmates!*"

This made Jada smile. She saw that the other kids must have given Pee Wee a chance.

"He has always been a charmer," she said quietly. Jada knew then that her little brother would overcome the situation.

At the end of school that day, when Pee Wee's mom arrived to pick them up, she spoke to Ms. Philips first.

"Hi, Ms. Philips. I heard Pee Wee had a rough couple of days," said Pee Wee's mom.

Ms. Philips replied, "Yes, I saw something was going on."

Pee Wee's mom went on to say, "Pee Wee told me that the other kids were teasing him, saying that he had 'cooties' which made him feel sad and left out."

"I'm so sorry that happened to Pee Wee," Ms. Philips said. "I can speak to the class if you would like."

Just as Ms. Philips and Pee Wee's mom were talking, Pee Wee came running out of school with the biggest smile on his face.

Voices in the crowd were saying, "Bye, Pee Wee!" and "See you tomorrow, Pee Wee!"

And Pee Wee shouted back, "Bye, guys!"

Pee Wee's mom and Ms. Philips saw all this, turned to each other, and Pee Wee's mom said, "Looks like today was a better day."

"Seems that way!" replied Ms. Philips with a smile.

Going home from school that day, Pee Wee couldn't help but smile as he looked out the car window.

While driving, Pee Wee's Mom asked, "How was your day, Pee Wee?"

"It was *great*!" he replied.

Jada chimed in, saying, "Yeah, I saw Pee Wee in the lunchroom talking with his classmates, having a good ol' time!"

Pee Wee looked at his mom and said, "You were right, Mom. Just be myself and talk about the things I like. Who knew I would have so much in common with the other kids!"

"Well, it's been a heck of a week, and it's not even Friday!" said Jada.

Everyone in the car laughed.

Later that night, as Pee Wee's mom and dad were tucking him into bed, his dad said, "So I hear you had a better day today at school, Pee Wee?"

"Yes, I did, Dad." Pee Wee went on to say, "I'm so happy because I was really feeling alone at first. It's pretty lonely when no one wants to be your friend and teases you. It made me want to disappear!"

Pee Wee's dad looked down at him and said, "You are never alone son, we're always here for you." Pee Wee's dad continues to say, "there's no disappearing, you have a purpose here on earth. We all do, there's a special plan written just for us. Everything we go through is preparing us to one day tell our story so that we can help others. Our experiences build our testimony. You're loving, smart, and strong. You are a sickle cell warrior, a **champion**! You can do anything you set your mind to. We believe in you Pee Wee, remember son if you ever need to talk, we're here for you."

Pee Wee's mom and dad then turned out his lights and said, "We love you, son, goodnight!"

"I love you too! Good night!"

With a heart full of love, Pee Wee fell asleep feeling more confident and stronger than ever. Prepared to take on whatever tomorrow may bring.

About the Author

The author grew up in San Diego, California. She struggled with having sickle cell disease. Growing up in the 70's and 80's, there wasn't much knowledge about sickle cell. Which made it difficult to navigate the world.

She went on to graduate from Samuel F. B. Morse High School. As an adult, she wanted to be there for the kids in the sickle cell community. She started volunteering at the Sickle Cell Disease Association of America San Diego Chapter.

After volunteering for a few years, she was voted as president of the association, where she stayed for over twelve years. Dealing with health issues of her own, she had to retire from the association. She never walked away from the community. She is still a sickle cell advocate and very present in the sickle cell community. She wanted to find a way to reach children around the world not just in her community. From her passion for the sickle cell community and her love for children, Pee Wee was born.